Puss in Boots

retold by Diane Stortz

Once there was a miller who had three sons. When the miller died, the oldest son became the owner of the mill, the middle son became the owner of the donkey, and the youngest son was left with only the cat.

"My brothers can grind wheat with the mill and take grain to market on the donkey," said the youngest son. "But whatever will I do with this cat?" The cat had never been good for anything more than catching mice.

The young man was feeling quite sorry for himself (which was foolish, considering what was about to happen).

"That's enough complaining," said the cat. "Get me some boots, and I will be able to help you." Surprised to hear the cat speak, the young man hurried off to the shoemaker's and came back with a pair of boots just the right size. The cat put them on and stood up. He was now Puss in Boots.

"Now I need a cloth sack with a cord at the top," said Puss in Boots. He filled the sack with grains of wheat and walked out of the house with the sack flung over his back. He went straight to the forest, where he opened the sack and laid it on the ground.

The cat hid behind a tree and waited. Soon, some fat partridges came by and wandered right into the sack. Quickly the cat pulled the sack shut and flung it over his shoulder again.

This time the cat went straight to the king's castle. He bowed low before the king and said, "My master, the Duke of Carabas, sends you his regards and these pretty partridges."

Now the king loved to eat partridges for supper. He had never heard of the Duke of Carabas (of course not--there was no such person). But he thanked Puss in Boots for the lovely present and told him to fill his sack with gold for his master.

The miller's son was amazed when he saw the gold.

Puss in Boots went hunting partridges every day after that. At the king's castle, he became a favorite guest...always allowed to make himself at home. One day, while lying by the hearth in the king's kitchen, he heard that the king and the princess would be taking a carriage ride around the lake that afternoon.

The cat ran home and said to his master, "Quick! You are going swimming!" By this time, the young man was more than happy to do whatever the cat told him. So he hurried to the lake, undressed, and jumped into the water. The cat took his clothes and hid them away.

Just then the king's carriage came into view. The cat stood by the side of the road and began to wail, "Oh, help! Help! My master is freezing. Someone stole his clothes while he was swimming in the lake and he cannot come out of the water."

The king recognized Puss in Boots and ordered the carriage to stop. One of his servants took a blanket to the miller's son, and another servant raced back to the castle for a suit of clothes.

When he was dry and dressed in the splendid clothes, the miller's son certainly looked like a duke. The king believed that he was the Duke of Carabas and invited the young duke to ride in the carriage, which pleased the princess. She was happy because the young man was so handsome.

Puss in Boots was very happy with the way events were working out. He ran ahead of the carriage: first to a wheat field, then to a meadow, and finally to a forest. In each place, he asked the workers there, "Who owns this land?" Each time the answer was the same: "The ogre, of course." "Well," said the cat. "The king is on his way here. When he asks you the same question, you must say that the owner is the Duke of Carabas. Otherwise the ogre will eat you."

All of the workers were afraid of the ogre and astonished by the cat. So when the king's carriage drove by, the king leaned out of the window and asked, "Who owns this land?" The workers answered him exactly as the cat had told them to do. The king and the princess were pleased to know that the young duke was so wealthy.

Puss in Boots ran on until he came to the ogre's castle. He walked right in and bowed to the ogre. "I have heard," said the cat, "that you can turn yourself into any animal at all. I'm sure you can turn yourself into something ordinary, like a dog or a fox, but I don't believe you can turn yourself into something spectacular, like a lion. I have to be convinced. Show me!"

The ogre was happy to do so. He became a lion so ferocious that even Puss in Boots was afraid--but only for a moment.

"A nice trick," said the cat. "But surely you cannot turn yourself into something very small, like a mouse."

"No problem at all," roared the ogre, and in an instant he was running around the room as a mouse. Puss in Boots had not caught any mice for quite a while, but he caught this one and ate him up with one gulp.

Just then, the cat heard the king's carriage approaching. He ran outside to welcome the king and the princess to the castle of his master, the Duke of Carabas.

The king was amazed by the magnificent building, almost more stunning than his own castle. The young man was amazed by what the cat had done for him.

The duke married the princess, and when the king died, the duke became king.

Puss in Boots was his chief advisor, with time off now and then for catching mice.